Disney's KIM POSSIBLE

attack of the KILLER BEBES

Adapted by Jim Pascoe

Based on the series created by

Mark McCorkle & Bob Schooley

Watch it on

Disney CHANNEL   abc Kids

Disney PRESS

VOLO

New York

Printed in the United States of America

First Edition
1 3 5 7 9 10 8 6 4 2

Library of Congress Catalog Card Number: 2003096536

ISBN 0-7868-4624-0
For more Disney Press fun, visit www.disneybooks.com
Visit DisneyChannel.com

CHAPTER 1

Stress Out

"No. No problem," said Ron Stoppable as he left the school counselor's office. "No, thank *you*."

The door closed, and Ron slid to the floor. "My life is *so* over," he muttered.

After school, Ron went to Bueno Nacho. But even his favorite place to chow down couldn't cheer him up.

"Ron," said his best friend, Kim Possible, "turn down the drama and eat."

"Not hungry," Ron said sadly.

Kim had never seen Ron in such a slump. He was *so* not having a good time.

Rufus, Ron's pet naked mole rat, jumped onto the table. Rufus was *always* hungry—

even if Ron wasn't! He rubbed his little paws together and dove right into Ron's burrito.

Chomp! Chomp! Chomp!

Ron was too sad to notice. "What am I gonna do, K.P.?" he asked.

"Well, let's see," said Kim. "The school counselor told you that you need an extracurricular activity."

"'Cause it'll look 'good' on my college applications," Ron said with a sigh. "That's *years* away!"

"There's plenty of teams and clubs out there," said Kim. "You could join . . . the Mathletes."

"Yeah, right," said Ron. "I can't get in that kind of shape."

Kim tried again. "How about the debate team?"

"Look, I'm not going to argue with you, Kim," said Ron.

"After-school activities are great," she told him, grabbing her pom-pom. "Like cheer squad for me."

Suddenly, Ron's eyes lit up. "Cheer squad!"

Kim dropped her pom-pom. Her jaw dropped, too. "For *me*. Not you," she said.

But Ron wasn't hearing her.

"That's it!" he cried. "I'm upbeat! I could do that."

"Do *what*?" Kim asked with worry.

"Cheerleader!" cried Ron. He grabbed her pom-pom. "Yeah! Go, Mad Dogs! Whoo-hoo!"

Ron felt happy again—and hungry. He was about to take a big bite of his burrito when a tiny mole rat head popped out.

Rufus had eaten every bit of the yummy bean filling!

But even an empty burrito couldn't get Ron down. *Boo-ya!* he thought. He was going to be a cheerleader!

CHAPTER 2

What's for Launch?

now it was Kim's turn to say—

"My life is *so* over."

She paced back and forth in the kitchen. This thing with Ron was going to be a total disaster. She was sure of it.

Her mother didn't agree. "I think it's cute that Ron wants to be a cheerleader."

"Mother, boy bands are *cute*. Brown bear backpacks are *cute*. Ron as a cheerleader—*not* cute," said Kim.

"He'll wear a different outfit, won't he?"

7

asked Kim's mom, dialing a phone number.

Kim pictured Ron in the squad's purple skirt and top. She shuddered, horrified.

Kim's mother spoke into the phone. "Hi, hon. Pizza for dinner. What do you want on yours?"

Kim's dad was on the other end of the line. He was a rocket scientist and a genius. He was also a bit clumsy.

"Hmm . . . toppings . . ." he said into the phone at the rocket lab. As he talked, he leaned back against one of the lab's control panels. He accidentally pressed a big red button.

Large numbers on his computer monitor began counting down.

Ten . . . nine . . . eight . . .

Dr. Possible didn't notice. He was too busy

talking about pizza. "Well, you know I love bacon on pretty much everything," he said.

Meanwhile, the numbers on his computer kept counting down.

. . . three . . . two . . . one . . . Liftoff!

Outside, a rocket roared off a launchpad.

Poor Dr. Possible had his back to the window. So he completely missed the takeoff.

"Okay, see you soon," he told Kim's mom. Then he turned around. His launchpad was as empty as his stomach!

"Ooh, gotta go," said Dr. Possible.

After he hung up, he began tapping on his

computer. Since his rocket had taken off, he figured he'd better track it!

Suddenly, his cell phone rang.

"Hello?" Dr. Possible answered.

"Hey, Possible!" the caller said. "Bob Chen here."

Professor Bob Chen was an old friend of Dr. Possible's. He studied the stars. So he spent most of his time at the Mount Middleton Observatory.

"Uh, listen," said Professor Chen, gazing

into a huge telescope. "Did you *launch* something over there?"

In the shadows behind Professor Chen, glowing red eyes appeared.

On the other end of the phone line, Dr. Possible said, "On the Q.T., Bob? Prototype

G-6 rocket just went up like a dream." Then he sighed and admitted, "Too bad it wasn't supposed to launch until next week."

Chen laughed. "Lean on a button again?"

Back at the observatory, another set of evil eyes appeared in the shadows.

"Roger that, Bob," confessed Dr. Possible.

Suddenly, a red beam scanned Bob Chen's body. He didn't even notice!

"So, will we see you at the class reunion this weekend?" Professor Chen asked.

"Wouldn't miss it," said Dr. Possible as he caught sight of some strange blips on his computer screen.

"Ouch," he said. "Looks like the military is scrambling around my rocket. Better hop off, Bob."

"See ya at the reunion, buddy," said Professor Chen. Then he hung up and laughed to himself. "Same old Possible."

That's when the creatures with red eyes closed in on the sky scientist. And Bob Chen's laughter turned into a scream.

CHAPTER 3

Who Let the Mad Dog Out?

Kim sat on a pink bench in the girls' locker room. Angry cheerleaders surrounded her. The angriest was Bonnie Rockwaller.

"You cannot allow this, Kim!" Bonnie cried.

Kim took a deep breath and tried to use her best "reasonable" voice.

"Bonnie," said Kim, "I'm as freaked out about this as you are. But there is no rule that says Ron can't try out."

Bonnie freaked some more. "Check your calendar," she snapped. "This is not 'Befriend a Loser' week."

"Ron is not a loser," said Kim quickly. "He's just . . . different."

Just then, the door to the girls' locker room cracked open. A boy's head popped in.

It was Ron!

He'd been hanging in the gym. But he was so excited about trying out, he just couldn't wait any longer.

"Hey, ladies, let's boogie!" he cried. He kept one hand over his eyes—just in case the girls were still changing.

Rufus ran down Ron's arm. "Oh, yeah," he squeaked and did a little boogie move.

But the cheerleaders were *not* ready to boogie. Especially not with Ron.

"Ladies?" asked Ron. With his eyes still

closed, he couldn't see Bonnie walking toward him or reaching toward the door.

Slam! The door banged shut. Ron was sent flying across the gym.

Fluff! He landed in a pile of pom-poms.

Ron looked at Rufus. This could only mean one thing, Ron decided. "They take a long time to get dressed!"

Rufus rubbed his head. "Hmmm."

Kim pushed through the locker room door and walked over to Ron. "Hey," she said.

Ron jumped up from the pom-pom pile.

"Where's the squad?" he said excitedly. "I'm pumped!"

"They, um, uh, they take a long time to get dressed," Kim said. Then she took a nervous breath and blurted out: "Are you totally sure you want to be a cheerleader, Ron?"

She was thinking: *Please say no, please say no, please say no!*

Ron laughed away her concern. "Oh, I'm not going to be a cheerleader, K.P."

Thank you, thank you, thank you! she thought. But what she said was, "You're not? Great! I mean, um, why not?"

"Because I'm going to be the"—Ron reached behind the pom-poms and pulled a huge dog mask over his head—"mascot! Middleton Mad Dogs bite!"

Ron jumped all around, throwing his hands in the air and barking like a . . . well, like a *mad dog*.

The locker room door swung open, and out came Bonnie.

Kim knew things were about to get ugly. She asked Ron, "Where did you get that mask?"

"I made it!" Ron said proudly as he slipped it off. He pointed to a large box of goop, gels, mirrors, and makeup. "With my Movie Magic Makeup kit."

An oversized mask of Kim Possible crawled out from behind the makeup kit. It squealed a familiar line. "What's the sitch?"

Kim yanked the mask up to reveal a laughing naked mole rat.

"I'm impressed . . ." Kim said, looking at her own likeness, ". . . and disturbed."

"Does it not rock hard? Check this out," said Ron. He pulled out a squirt ball attached to a tube inside the mask. Then he whipped the mad dog's face back on.

"Mad Dog foams at the mouth!" he yelled while shaking his head back and forth. The more he pumped the ball, the more foam spewed out of his mangy mascot mouth.

Sploorsh! Foam flew all over the gym. Large globs landed on Kim and Bonnie.

Bonnie screamed, "Kim!"

Kim screamed, "Ron!"

They were furious, but Ron was clueless. He thought Kim and Bonnie *liked* the mask.

"The crowd will eat it up!" said Ron. "Taste it! It's banana cream."

The foamy cream dripped off Kim's face. There was a bad taste in her mouth, and it *wasn't* banana cream.

"Yum," said Kim, through an angry frown.

Rufus ran over to Bonnie. He scampered up her leg and licked the cream off her arm. *Sluuuurp!*

Bonnie was outraged. She pulled Rufus off and held him up by the tail.

"This idea is idiotic," said Bonnie. "The entire student body will laugh at you."

"But—" Ron started to say.

"Not *with* you. *At* you," snapped Bonnie. Then she threw little Rufus back at Ron.

"Look—" Ron said, catching his flying friend.

"Loudly and cruelly. They will laugh," Bonnie said.

"You don't deserve to be kissed by a naked mole rat," Ron said.

Rufus grunted in agreement.

Kim stood in the middle of the two, which

was exactly where she did *not* want to be. "Ron—" she began.

"I know, Kim, I know," he said. "You believe in me, and you'll work on them."

"Um, I . . . I kind of *agree* with *Bonnie*," she told him.

"Oh," said Ron. For a second, he couldn't believe what was happening. He looked back and forth between Kim and Bonnie.

"Oh, I see," he finally said.

But what Ron couldn't "see" was why his friend—his very *best* friend—had just stabbed him in the back.

CHAPTER 4

A Blast from Dad's Past

"**D**ad? I have a problem," Kim said.

Her dad looked up nervously from his newspaper. He was great at figuring out math problems, but girl problems—forget it.

"Frankly, uh, your *mother* has the good advice vis-à-vis boy trouble," he said.

"Oh, this isn't about a boy," said Kim. "It's about Ron."

"Oh. Got ya." Her dad set his paper aside.

"Everyone got down on Ron today and,

22

uh, I don't know. Maybe I should have stuck up for him."

"But you didn't?" her dad said.

"He was foaming at the mouth!" cried Kim. "I'm only human."

Dr. Possible smiled at Kim's reaction. "Well, you know, Kimmie, back when I was in college, I had a group of friends. My, uh, my 'posse,' if you will."

Kim tried not to cringe. Her dad was *so* uncool.

"It was the night of the big science department mixer," her dad went on. "In those days, I wasn't exactly a ladies' man. . . ."

Many years ago, the young Dr. Possible couldn't get a date for his big college party. Neither could his three best friends, Drew, Bob, and Ramesh.

A few weeks before the party, Drew announced he would get all four of them dates. But, on the night of the party, Drew was nowhere to be found.

"Where's Drew?" young Dr. Possible asked Bob and Ramesh. "He was supposed to be here a half hour ago!"

Young Bob Chen—the future star man—sighed. "I knew he wouldn't come through with dates for us."

"What did you expect?" said Ramesh. "He cannot even come through with a date for himself."

"This was folly," Chen said.

"It was a nice dream, though," said the young Dr. Possible.

Just then, the door creaked open. A voice boomed through the computer room: "The dream is real."

The voice belonged to a scrawny kid with glasses.

"Drew!" cried Bob Chen, bubbling with nerdy excitement. "You found girls!"

"Found?" said Drew, laughing at the idea. He had something much bigger in mind.

"Gentlemen, tonight we make history. I give you . . . the future!"

Drew's friends waited for "the future" to enter. They were hoping "the future" would be four cute girls.

What entered instead looked like washing machines with wigs!

Four big, bulky robots rolled into the room. Sparks jumped off their blue, barrel-shaped bodies. One of them spoke in a mechanical voice. "My name is Bebe."

Drew's friends gasped in horror.

But Drew didn't notice. Instead, he bowed like a gentleman in front of the robo-dates.

"Bebe, would you like to dance?" he asked.

"Affirmative. Bebe will dance," said the robot.

Young Dr. Possible watched the robot dance with Drew. For a moment, he wasn't sure whether Bebe was dancing or trying to twist Drew into a pretzel.

Zum, zum, zum!

She spun him around. Then she hugged him like a pro wrestler.

"As gentle as a summer shower, no?" Drew croaked.

27

"No," all three classmates said. Then they burst out laughing. "The future" may not have been cute, but it sure was funny.

Little did Bob, Ramesh, and young Dr. Possible know that Drew the young scientist was well on his way to becoming Drew the *mad* scientist.

"All right. Go on, laugh away," roared Drew angrily. "But one day my genius will be recognized! Bebe will be perfect!"

Bebe squeezed him tighter. In a high voice, he squeaked, "And *I* will be the one laughing!"

Then Bebe's voice screeched—"I am Bebe"—and her robo-head popped off.

* * *

Kim finished listening to her dad's story about his college days.

"Drew dropped out, and we never saw him again," said Dr. Possible. "I don't think he ever forgave us. And, in some small way, maybe we never forgave ourselves."

"For just a giggle fit?" Kim asked.

"No, no, Kimmie. We laughed for *days* . . . long and loud, with youthful abandon."

"Oh," Kim said. "That was bad."

"So you'll reconsider Ronald's dream?"

Kim rolled her eyes. Parents were all the same. They just *did not* get it.

"I don't think so," she said. "His Mad Dog routine is way stupid."

CHAPTER 5

We Have Come for You

Ron slammed his locker door shut. Hard.

"Well, that's one person's opinion!" he yelled.

Kim corrected him: "One entire cheerleading squad's opinion."

Ron pulled out his Mad Dog mask and shoved it in her face. "Well, maybe you and your squad just don't get it."

Kim yelled back, "*You* don't get it."

Ron lay the Mad Dog mask down and put

the Kim mask on his head. "Oh, I'm Kim Possible. I can do anything . . . except believe in my best friend!"

Ron tugged the mask back off. He couldn't remember ever having been this mad at Kim.

Rufus stuck his tiny tongue out at Kim. *Ppppffffttttt!*

What was this, Kim thought—*junior* high?

Kim's Kimmunicator chirped. She tapped on the screen and said, "Go, Wade."

Wade was Kim's tech-head friend who ran her Web site. When he called, it usually meant someone was in trouble.

"I've got a weird one," he said.

Kim saw that Ron was standing there with his back to her. "Me, too," she said.

"Professor Ramesh from the Mount Middleton Observatory wants your help," Wade reported.

"That name sounds familiar," Kim said. "I think my dad knows him."

"Ramesh's partner, Professor Chen, is missing," said Wade.

"Okay, Wade," said Kim. "Set up a ride. I'll bring the man of a thousand faces."

"No, thanks. I'll fly solo," said Ron.

Rufus grunted in agreement. This naked mole rat was definitely on Ron's side.

"Nice going, Possible," Kim muttered to herself. Finding missing scientists was easy, compared to arguing with your best bud. *That* was way hard.

* * *

A little while later, near Mount Middleton Observatory, a TV news helicopter landed on the lawn.

The pilot spoke into his headset: "—And that's the traffic update from your Eye over Middleton."

The copter door opened, and Kim stepped out. "Thanks for the lift, Dallas," she said to the pilot.

The beefy newsman smiled at Kim. "Well, it's the least I could do after you brought that interstate police chase to a happy end."

"No big," she said. "The guy didn't even know he needed a new brake light."

Kim pulled out her Kimmunicator to check on Ron.

"Ron? Come in, Ron," Kim said. "Ron!"

Finally, Ron's voice came in. "Sorry . . . *kkzzzz* . . . can't hear . . . *kkzzzz* . . . you . . . *kkzzzz*."

Kim could totally tell that he was making that stupid static noise himself. Boys, she thought with a sigh.

On the other end of the line, Ron pedaled his bike up a steep hill. "Bad . . . *kkzzzz* . . . reception . . . *kkzzzz* . . . uh . . . *kkzzzz*." In

between deep breaths and snickering, he kept up with the bogus static sounds.

"Come off it, Ron," Kim said. "I know you're doing that yourself."

"What?" Ron continued his lame-o attempt at fooling Kim. "I'm only . . . *kkzzzz* . . . hearing . . . *kkzzzz* . . . every . . . *kkzzzz* . . . other . . . *kkzzzz* . . . word."

Kim gave it right back to him. "Ron, don't be such a . . ."—Kim blew air and spit threw her teeth to mock Ron's static: "*Kkzzthhhpppt* . . . baby!"

Just then, a loud crash boomed through the night.

* * *

Inside the observatory, Professor Ramesh tried to hide behind his smashed equipment.

"Stay back!" he yelled as three shadows came toward him.

"Professor Ramesh . . ." said a computerized voice. It belonged to one of three blond robotic girls. Their blue metal skin looked cold and unfriendly. Their eyes glowed an evil red. But nevertheless, these girls—they were *cute*.

They marched forward.

"We have . . ." said one Bebe.

". . . come for . . ." said another Bebe.

". . . you," said the third killer Bebe.

Blue Bots

Professor Ramesh tried to get away, but there was no escaping these wicked blue beauties.

"Who—who are you?" he stammered.

Zummazummazumm!

The killer Bebes shook like an engine ready to explode. The professor turned and ran for the exit. Suddenly, one of the killer robots zoomed over to block his exit.

"I am Bebe," she said.

Zoooom! Another came and blocked the scared scientist. She said, "I am Bebe."

Zoooom! Number three said, "I am Bebe."

The door to the observatory slammed open. The Bebes all twisted around to see Kim Possible striking a pose in the doorway.

"Is there an echo in here?" Kim asked.

The Bebes' mechanical eyes scanned Kim. They all spoke their report: "Analysis. Subject: Kim Possible. Threat: minimal."

Kim pouted. "That hurts."

She ran toward them, crouched into a handspring flip, and then launched into a flying kick. But Bebe number one was a bit too fast—she caught Kim's ankle and whipped her across the science center.

No big, thought Kim.

She caught herself on the huge telescope and swung down to safety, dropping into a fight stance. Then she held up her fists and said, "Not bad."

All three robots raised their right arms and spoke.

"Bebe . . ."

". . . is . . ."

". . . perfect."

Then their arms shot out like snakes and attacked Kim.

Slam! Kim ducked, as an arm smashed into the computer behind her. *Slam!* Another arm pounded beside her.

Whoa, thought Kim, these chicks aren't playing! Kim bounced onto an office chair and rolled across the room. Then she grabbed

Professor Ramesh, and together they raced toward the door.

Zummazummazumm!

The Bebes zoomed after them. Kim and the professor ran for the front entrance. The Bebes were too fast for her.

The three Bebes had Kim and Ramesh surrounded. The robots' blue bodies twisted into creepy spider forms.

As the Bebes crawled toward them, Kim said to Ramesh, "What *are* they?"

Then came a sound so unexpected, so strange, so silly, that everyone turned to look at the front door.

Dingalingaling! It was Ron's bicycle bell. And with it came Ron to the rescue.

Unfortunately, he had not yet noticed the killer Bebes.

"Kim . . ." he panted as he pedaled the bike up to her. "Don't think I didn't . . . hear that . . . *baby* comment. I heard it!"

He tried to catch his breath. That's when he noticed a blue-skinned, spider-shaped robot of pure evil crawling toward him.

His eyes popped out of his head. His jaw hung open. *Boom!* He was on the ground, totally passed out.

"Ron!" Kim cried out. She stepped away from the professor to help her friend.

That was the one chance the Bebes needed. *Snatch!* They scooped up Professor Ramesh, and—*zoom!*—they were gone.

Kim finally gave Ron a helping hand— along with a handful of attitude. "Thanks a lot!" she snapped.

"What did I do?" Ron said.

"Yeah!" Rufus squawked from on top of Ron's shoulder.

"Those robots took Professor Ramesh," said Kim. "Are you happy now?"

"Yes!" cried Ron, more than a little tweaked.

"Mm-hmm," Rufus agreed.

Ron thought for a second. "I mean, no!"

Rufus waved his paws. "Uh-uh. Uh-uh. Uh-uh."

Kim threw up her hands. "Whatever," she said. "All I know is that now we've got two missing scientists and three killer Bebes."

And with that, she stormed off.

CHAPTER 7

The Secret Mission

As Ron started to chase after Kim, he heard a crunching sound on the ground. He lifted his foot up and saw that he had planted a shoe in a fallen picture frame.

Ron bent down to pick up the pic.

"Huh? Professor Ramesh . . ." said Ron, looking at it.

In the picture, a young Professor Ramesh stood with two friends. "Back in the old college days," Ron said to Rufus. "Check it out."

Rufus squinted his naked mole rat eyes at the old photo. "Hmmm?" he said, pointing at one of Ramesh's friends.

"Oh, yeah," Ron said. "That guy must be Professor Chen!"

Rufus jumped up and down, pointing at the *other* friend.

"What? No way. That is not—" Ron's eyes bulged when he looked more closely at the third college student. "Wow! It is! It's Kim's dad!"

Ron rubbed his chin. "Oh, this is terrible!"

Rufus nodded his head.

"I mean, can you believe he actually wore

his jacket that way—with the sleeves pushed up? Totally eighties!" Ron shuddered at the thought of looking that uncool.

Rufus growled. As far as the naked mole rat could see, Ron was acting uncool in the *head*. Rufus pointed at Chen, then at Ramesh, then frantically at Kim's dad.

Ron's eyes glazed over just like they did when he was in math class. The wheels in his head turned *slooooowly*.

Rufus kept pointing. *Kim's dad. Kim's dad. Kim's dad.*

Finally, the wheels in Ron's head went

click! "Kim's dad could be the next target," he said.

Rufus sighed with relief.

Ron slammed the photo to his chest, crushing Rufus, who let out a muffled cry.

"Gotta tell Kim—" Ron said. "No. Wait. We don't need Kim."

As Ron relaxed his hold on the picture, Rufus unflattened himself.

"I know exactly what to do!" Ron snapped his helmet back on and rode his bike out of Mount Middleton Observatory.

The next morning, the killer Bebes were hiding on the roof of Kim Possible's house.

Patiently, they waited until Kim's dad walked out of the house and down to the driveway.

"Subject: Dr. Possible," they chanted. "Directive: capture."

Kim's dad climbed into his car. As he turned the key, he thought he heard something. Suddenly, three blue fists punched through the metal roof of his car!

"We have come for you," the Bebes said as they reached out and grabbed him.

Meanwhile, in the high school gym, Kim and her cheerleading squad were practicing a new routine. It was guaranteed to fire up the Mad Dog fans.

Just as the squad landed in a perfect pyramid formation, the gym doors slammed open. In walked Kim's dad.

"Kimberly Ann Possible!" he roared.

Kim froze with embarrassment. "Dad? Here?"

Bonnie—never one to miss a dis—said, "Oh, great. Kim found *another* new recruit for the squad."

Kim tossed up her pom-poms and ran to hug her dad. "Daddy, hi!" she said, sweetly. "What are you doing here?"

But her dad was still sour. "Where's Ronald?"

"Not here," Kim said, turning to show her dad the Ron-less squad.

Bonnie began tapping her foot impatiently on the wood floor.

Kim's dad rubbed the back of his neck.

"Well, that hole in the roof of my car really grinds my beans!"

Kim began shuffling her dad off toward the exit. "I'll be sure that Ron gets the message—wait a second. He put a hole in your car roof?"

"He came over to the house," Dr. Possible explained. "Said something about a mission."

Oh, no, Kim thought, then gulped. "What mission?"

Somewhere across town in a dark room, Professor Chen, Professor Ramesh, and a smiling Dr. Possible decoy were being held captive.

Glowing green rings surrounded them, making a dangerous electric cage.

The three killer Bebes stood guard.

"Who's behind this?" Ramesh asked.

Chen had an answer. "It's obvious. Some villain needs our genius to help take over the world. What else could it be?"

A shadowy figure entered the room. He had blue skin, a nasty scar on his cheek, and a horrible, out-of-style ponytail.

He spoke: "Gentlemen, don't flatter yourselves. There's only one 'genius' in this room, and it is I, Doctor Drakken."

Drakken was Kim Possible's archenemy. He was also an old college buddy of the men standing before him.

"Drew?" Professor Chen asked.

"Drew Lipsky?" Professor Ramesh echoed. "Is that you?"

Dr. Possible was still smiling a rubbery smile— that's because he *was* rubber! He ripped off the rubber mask he wore.

Underneath the mask was Ron Stoppable.

"No," yelled Ron, "it's Doctor Drakken, and he's in for a world of hurt!"

Seeing Ron, Drakken's face turned a paler shade of blue. "So," he said, "Kim Possible is near!"

Ron threw the mask at Drakken. "Oh, yes!"

Chen and Ramesh were overjoyed.

Then Ron spilled the truth. "Actually, no."

Chen and Ramesh were now definitely *under*joyed.

Doctor Drakken, however, was in mad-scientist heaven.

CHAPTER 8

Strange Reunion

Kim and her dad drove through the streets of Middleton. The car ride was a little breezy, mostly because there was a large hole in the roof.

Kim clicked a button on her Kimmunicator. "Wade, Ron's missing. Can you find him?" she asked.

Wade's face appeared on the screen. "Do you think I have him microchipped or something?"

"Well, do you?" she asked hopefully.

"Yeah. Hang on," he said.

Wade's face was replaced on the screen of the Kimmunicator with a map of Middleton. The map had a blinking light on it—Ron's location.

Back in the dark room, Drakken paced in front of his three Bebes.

"You know," he grumbled, "I purposely programmed you with a pinch of human emotion, just so you would be ashamed of failures like this."

Drakken waved Ron's mask in front of

their blue faces. "It's slipshod, is what it is!" he cried.

"Slipshod?" one Bebe said.

"That's right, missy," Drakken barked. "And I demand better from my lackeys. Especially the robotic ones!"

Now, all three of the Bebes showed some emotion. It was called anger. "Lackey?" they said in unison.

"Ah, let's not get testy. I am a patient man. You will get another chance. Go forth and find Dr. Possible!" cried Drakken.

Zoooom! Just like that, the Bebes were gone.

Ron scratched his head. "Why are you after Kim's dad and his friends, anyway?"

Drakken spun around. "Payback! For you see—" He stopped. "Wait. You mean Dr. Possible and Kim Possible are *related*?"

"Duh," Ron said.

"Don't 'duh' me," Drakken snapped. "Possible is a very common last name."

"So *not*," said Ron.

"So . . . so, yes, it is," said Drakken.

"It's pretty unique," Ron said.

"Enough!" Drakken screamed. "I shall prove it!" He looked all around, mumbling, "Where's the phone book?"

* * *

Outside, Kim and her dad drove up to the Middleton Motor Lodge. The parking attendant was draped over the valet stand.

Kim's dad got out of the car and said, "Uh, park it close. We shouldn't be long."

The valet's eyes were closed. He responded with a big zzzzzzzzzzzzz!

Kim said, "Keep your keys, Dad. This guy's been hit with knockout gas."

Inside, the scene was grim. *Everyone* was knocked out.

"This is bad," Kim said.

"I'll say," her dad agreed. "They'd better get this ironed out before our big college reunion this weekend."

Kim kept marching forward, looking for Ron and the professors. What she didn't notice was Dr. Drakken behind the front desk. He had found a phone book. *Flip! Flip! Flip!* through the pages he went.

Kim and her dad walked into a large, dark room. Kim hit the light switch on the wall.

They found themselves in a banquet hall, all decorated. One banner read WELCOME,

SCIENTISTS. Other banners had pictures of beakers and atomic symbols.

Very hip, thought Kim. *Not!*

In the center of the room was a holding pen of glowing green rings. Inside were Ron, Chen, and Ramesh.

"Kim!" Ron shouted. "It was Drakken!"

"Drakken's behind this?" said Kim. She knew Dr. Drakken was demented, but this was *so* unlike his usual take-over-the-world thing.

The mad scientist marched right past Kim and her father. He didn't see them

because his head was buried in a phone book.

"Okay, fine," Drakken muttered. "So, in Middleton there's only *one* Possible family."

"Duh," Kim said.

Drakken dropped the book and spun around. "Kim Possible!" he cried. "And . . . and—"

Ron rolled his eyes. "Her father, Dr. Possible," he said.

Drakken turned to Ron and snapped, "Yes. Well, there's no way I could be expected to conclude that my archnemesis is really the daughter of a guy I went to college with."

Dr. Possible scratched his head. "Drew?" he said. "Drew Lipsky?"

Kim's brain was going into major overload. "Wait. *He's* the guy from your college?" she asked her dad. "My archfoe?"

"Well," her dad said, "he didn't used to be *blue*. I can tell you that much."

Drakken got all sappy. "Oh, but I *was* blue—on the inside. Scorned by my so-called friends . . . my . . . my *posse*." He shook off his sappiness and returned to full-on crazy. "But I vowed to prove my genius to all of you. And when I got the reunion invite—"

Drakken pulled out a paper invitation. Dr. Possible snatched it from Drakken's hand.

"Since you dropped out, you're not really entitled to that," Kim's dad said.

"Indeed." Drakken scowled. "Exactly why I planned my *own* little reunion. Bebes, return to me at once!"

Zoooom! Just like that, the Bebes were lined up in the banquet hall.

Dr. Drakken paraded in front of his creations. "Ha-ha! Who's the genius now?" he cackled. "These robots are perfect! And their sole purpose is to obey me!"

The Bebes' eyes flared. They began questioning their master one by one.

"Question: if we are . . ." one Bebe said.

". . . perfect . . ." another Bebe said.

". . . why do we obey . . ."

". . . one who is *not* perfect . . . ?"

Then all of the killer Bebes said at once: "Conclusion: Dr. Drakken is unfit to command."

Drakken's face fell when he realized his Bebes had gone bad.

Inside the holding circle, Chen chuckled and elbowed his buddy, Ramesh. "It's college all over again," he said. "That man can*not* build a robot."

Ramesh just shook his head. "He should take up cloning."

Drakken backed away from his Bebes,

waving his hands and begging for mercy. "Bebes! No! Bad Bebes! Bad!"

Kim shook her head and handed the Kimmunicator to her dad. "This is just too weird."

With a running start, Kim jumped up and pushed off Drakken's shoulders. She did a giant backflip in the air and landed on the shoulders of two Bebes. It was just like a cheerleading pyramid, except Kim reached down and smashed the two Bebes' heads together. Sparks flew.

"Whoa," Professor Ramesh said to Dr. Possible. "Where did your little Kimmie learn to kick bottom like that?"

"Cheerleading," Kim's dad said with a proud smile.

Kim pumped her fist in the air. "Yes!" With two broken Bebes, Kim was thinking this was going to be way easy. She leaped off the robots' shoulders—and right into the arms of Bebe number three.

Correction, thought Kim: way *not* easy.

Kim smiled up at Bebe, but Bebe did not smile back. Instead, the evil robot threw Kim across the room.

"Kim!" shouted Dr. Possible.

The fight was far from over. It had just begun.

CHAPTER 9

Many Geniuses, One Solution

The battle rumbled on.

Reunion name tags flew everywhere as one Bebe picked up a big table and threw it. Kim barely escaped being hit.

The other two Bebes got their heads working and joined the table-throwing Bebe.

Zummazummazumm! In an instant they had Kim surrounded.

Kim grabbed a microphone stand from the banquet hall's stage. She twirled it like a ninja weapon. Then she swung it at a Bebe. *Snap!* Bebe blocked the blow.

"Wha?" Kim grunted, looking at her makeshift weapon. It was broken in half!

The Bebes continued to attack, punching their fists into the floor and through the walls. Each time, Kim barely avoided getting smashed.

"Ah!" Kim's dad let out a worried gasp.

The Bebes kept coming at Kim, faster and harder. She ducked a punch. "Ah!" she gasped. Then another. "Ah!" she gasped even louder.

One of the robots clamped down on Kim's

wrist and lifted her up like a trophy fish.

Ron couldn't take it anymore. "We've got a roomful of geniuses here!" he yelled. "Can't somebody come up with something!"

"Don't look at me," said Professor Chen. "I'm an astronomer."

Professor Ramesh shrugged, too. "Ditto."

Ron glared at Dr. Drakken. "And you?" he asked.

"Let the ladies work this out among themselves," said Drakken.

Two normal geniuses and one evil genius down, thought Ron. One to go. Ron had high hopes. Not only was Dr. Possible a genius, he

was also Kim's dad. And sometimes, dads were the smartest guys in the world.

Kim's dad pushed a button on Kim's Kimmunicator. "Wade," he called.

"Dr. Possible?" Wade answered.

"I need a sonic disturbance," Dr. Possible ordered. "Make it loud. Make it ultrahigh frequency."

"Something that can jam a wireless network signal?" Wade asked.

Kim's dad responded with a smile. "Please and thank you," he said.

One of the killer Bebes was still holding Kim up by the wrist. Kim grunted from the pain. Then, suddenly, she heard the noise.

Eeeeeeeeeeeeeeeeeeeeeeeeeeeee!

The Bebes heard it too. Their red eyes scanned the room. They saw Ron and the scientists plugging their ears. And they saw Dr. Possible holding the Kimmunicator up high.

The Bebes all said, "Analysis. Subject: Dr. Possible's attack strategy. Threat: substantial."

Sparks shot out of the robots' bodies. Static filled the air. "Destroy electronic device," they warbled.

Thud! They dropped Kim to the ground and staggered toward Kim's dad.

"Huh?" he said when he realized they were now after *him*! He turned and ran.

But he wasn't fast enough.

The Bebes surrounded him.

"Dr. P.!" Ron shouted, sticking his hands out of his prison. "I'm open!"

Kim's dad threw the Kimmunicator to Ron.

Zoooom! All three Bebes lunged for the device. One snatched it right before it reached Ron's fingers.

But the other two Bebes couldn't stop! *Zoooom!* They plowed into the first Bebe. And all three fell into the glowing green rings.

Zap! Pow!

Electric sparks filled the hall. The Kimmunicator, still screeching, went skating across the floor. It landed right in front of Dr. Drakken.

His evil eyes went bright as he bent down to grab it. But Drakken was too late: Kim dove past him, and scooped it up first.

She got to her feet and held out the Kimmunicator toward the killer Bebes.

Eeeeeeeeeeeeeeeeeeeeeeeeeeeeeee!

The robots could barely stand up. One of them said, "Hive mind command . . ."

". . . connection . . ." another continued.

". . . l-l-l-lost," finished the third.

"I'll take that as good news," Kim said, tossing the Kimmunicator to her dad.

He yelled over the loud tone, "Now, Kim, you know I don't approve of violence, but they are deadly robots. You go, girl!"

And with a swift move, Kim went over and kicked some bolt.

When she was done, all that was left was smoke and broken robot parts.

"Way to go, Kim!" Ron cheered. "You too, Doctor P.!"

Kim's dad was still yelling over the tone. "What was that, Ronald?"

Kim took back the Kimmunicator and shut off the noise. She said, "Way to go, Dad."

Over near the exit, someone yelled, "Ah!" Dr. Drakken had stubbed his toe on a broken Bebe while trying to escape.

Kim did a flip and landed in front of him.

"What about your college reunion, *Drew*?" she said.

He said smugly, "I'll come to the next one—when I'm even more successful."

Drakken had one last trick up his sleeve. He pressed a button on his belt. Out popped a rocket pack! He laughed like a madman as the rockets lifted him up, up, up. . . .

And—*wham!*—right into the ceiling.

"Ow," Drakken whimpered. "Little help."

CHAPTER 10

Majorly Mad Dog

Kim's dad, Professor Chen, and Professor Ramesh sat around the Possible kitchen table. Kim's mom brought out a pizza.

"I can't believe Drew Lipsky turned into a mad scientist," said Kim's mom.

"Let alone our daughter's archnemesis," added Kim's dad.

Bob Chen gave a friendly elbow to Dr. Possible. "But my man knew what to do," he said.

Ramesh gave his own shout-out: "Possible," he said, "you rock."

"Oh, please." Dr. Possible waved away the praise. "Drakken was so obvious. I mean, really, the whole Bebe/bee theme. The hive-mind behavior was clearly the result of a cybertronic linkage through a wireless network."

Chen and Ramesh looked at each other and shrugged. "Uh . . . sure."

Kim's dad grabbed a slice of pizza. "Poor Drew," he said. "Maybe if we hadn't laughed at him back then, there would be one less mad scientist running around."

Kim was standing in the kitchen doorway, listening. She was happy her mad scientist problem was solved, but she still had a *Mad Dog* problem on her plate.

She turned and walked into the family room. Ron was on the floor, holding his Mad Dog mask.

Kim sat down on the sofa.

"The fact that I was so rotten to you," she told Ron, "that's not going to drive you to become some kind of mask-wearing villain, is it?"

"If I said *yes*, would you let me do my Mad Dog routine?"

"That's not a good reason for me to say *yes*," said Kim.

"I know," he said quietly.

"Because you're my best friend," Kim said with a smile. "*That's* a good reason."

"Boo-ya!" Ron jumped to his feet and pulled on the mask. "Mad Dog lives!"

He barked and howled with joy.

Later, at the big game, the Mad Dogs made a final basket right before halftime, putting them ahead: 32 to 30.

The buzzer sounded off, and the cheer-leaders strutted their stuff on the court. Then

the announcer cried, "Please, put your hands together for your Middleton Mad Dog!"

The lights went down, spotlights danced around, and out of the locker room doors ran Ron—dressed as the Mad Dog mascot.

He danced and pranced and barked and cheered. Ron had found his extracurricular activity, all right. And the crowd went wild.

"They like him?" Bonnie said in disbelief.

"Yeah," Kim said. "Kinda surprises me, too."